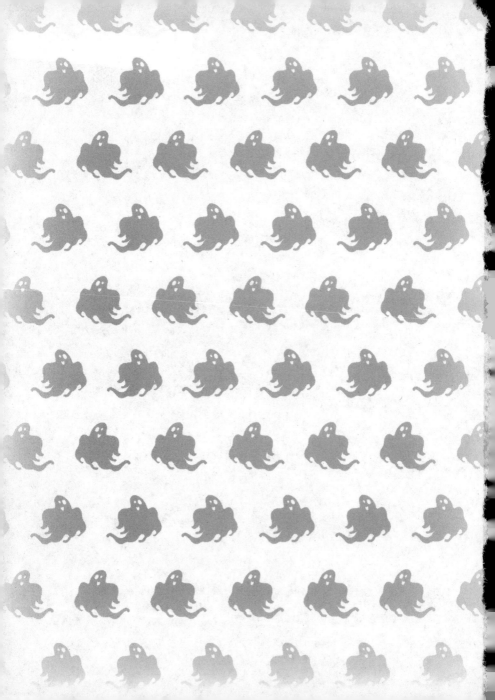

DESMOND COLE
GHOST PATROL
I'M YOUR BIGGEST PHANTOM

by **Andres Miedoso**
illustrated by **Victor Rivas**

LITTLE SIMON
New York   London   Toronto   Sydney   New Delhi

LITTLE SIMON

An imprint of Simon & Schuster Children's Publishing Division
1230 Avenue of the Americas, New York, New York 10020
First Little Simon paperback edition July 2024
Copyright © 2024 by Simon & Schuster, LLC
Also available in a Little Simon hardcover edition.
All rights reserved, including the right of reproduction in whole or in part in any form.
LITTLE SIMON is a registered trademark of Simon & Schuster, LLC, and associated colophon
is a trademark of Simon & Schuster, LLC.
Simon & Schuster: Celebrating 100 Years of Publishing in 2024
For information about special discounts for bulk purchases, please contact
Simon & Schuster Special Sales at 1-866-506-1949 or business@simonandschuster.com.
The Simon & Schuster Speakers Bureau can bring authors to your live event.
For more information or to book an event contact the Simon & Schuster Speakers Bureau
at 1-866-248-3049 or visit our website at www.simonspeakers.com.
Designed by Steve Scott
Manufactured in the United States of America 0624 LAK
2 4 6 8 10 9 7 5 3 1
Library of Congress Cataloging-in-Publication Data
Names: Miedoso, Andres, author. | Rivas, Victor, illustrator.
Title: I'm your biggest phantom / by Andres Miedoso ; illustrated by Victor Rivas.
Other titles: I am your biggest phantom
Description: First Little Simon paperback edition. | New York : Little Simon, 2024. | Series: Desmond Cole
ghost patrol ; book 22 | Audience: Ages 5–9. | Summary: Ghost Patrol's Andres and Desmond gain celebrity
status from the new kid in Kersville, but there is more behind his adoration than meets the eye.
Identifiers: LCCN 2023043856 (print) | LCCN 2023043857 (ebook) | ISBN 9781665952965 (paperback)
ISBN 9781665952972 (hardcover) | ISBN 9781665952989 (ebook)
Subjects: CYAC: Fans (Persons)—Fiction. | Ghosts—Fiction. | Friendship—Fiction. | LCGFT: Ghost stories.
Classification: LCC PZ7.1.M518 Im 2024 (print) | LCC PZ7.1.M518 (ebook) | DDC [Fic]—dc23
LC record available at https://lccn.loc.gov/2023043856
LC ebook record available at https://lccn.loc.gov/2023043857

CONTENTS

CHAPTER ONE

EVERY STAR HAS A STORY

Have you ever wondered what it's like to be a superstar?

If you were a star, you could ride in limousines, wear fancy clothes, and smile for pictures on the red carpet.

At the end of the day, you would go home to your huge mansion.

Imagine living in a home with a private movie theater *and* thirteen bathrooms!

I know, I know, you're probably thinking, *no one needs thirteen bathrooms*. But superstars do!

When you're a famous person, you also have fans. They're the ones who want to meet you so bad that they will wait in a long, snaking line that feels like it's going to last forever! But your fans won't mind waiting, because they like you *that* much.

Not only do fans like you, but some fans know everything about you! They even know your favorite animal and what you ate for dinner yesterday.

Me? I love porcupines, and I ate rice and beans with plantains last night. Just in case you wanted to know!

I bet you're wondering how I know so much about superstars and fans. Well, believe it or not, I was once a famous celebrity. I even signed some autographs! But things didn't turn out the way I thought they would.

As a matter of fact, that's me, Andres Miedoso, and my best friend, Desmond Cole. Yep, we're the ones hiding in that huge crowd.

I'm the one in the wide-brimmed hat and sunglasses. And Desmond is the one wearing the fake mustache and the crab costume.

ANDRES MIEDOSO

DESMOND COLE

You might not have noticed us right away because, shhh, we're in hiding . . . from our very own fan!

Why did we end up on the run from our greatest admirer? Well, keep reading.

They say every star has a story to tell, and I'm no different. This story is mine.

CHAPTER TWO

THIS TOWN IS SO WEIRD

It all started on a blazing hot Sunday in Kersville. My parents took Desmond and me to Dreary Beach.

I know you're thinking that's a pretty strange name for a beach. It *is*, in fact, a pretty strange beach, so the name makes sense!

We found a good spot on the sand and set up our blankets and beach umbrellas.

Desmond looked around. "Where's the rest of your stuff?" he asked.

When Desmond's family went to Dreary Beach, they packed their car with so many things, you would think they were going on a two-week

trip! It always took them FOREVER to unpack everything.

Just then a boy ran out of the water, screaming, "Run for your lives!"

He ran over to us and pointed toward the water. "Th-those surfers," he stammered. "They're not human!"

Desmond and I looked over at the water. And sure enough, there was a group of mersurfers floating around, waiting for the next big wave.

Oh yeah, if I hadn't mentioned it already, there are mersurfers at Dreary Beach. They are nice, as long as you treat the beach respectfully.

"This town is so weird!" the boy said, shaking. There were tears welling up in his eyes.

"You must be new to Kersville," Desmond said.

"How did you know?" the boy asked. "Are you a mind reader? Do you already know everything about me? Like, that my name is Stanley and I have five pet rocks?"

We shook our heads. We didn't need to be mind readers. We just knew Kersville wasn't exactly an ordinary town. Kersville had vampires, ghouls, monsters, demons, and werewolves. I even had a ghost named Zax living in my house!

Desmond waved to the mersurf-ers, and they waved back. Then he told Stanley, "If you ever have any trouble here in Kersville, the Ghost Patrol can help."

He pulled a business card out of
the pocket of his swim shorts and
handed it to Stanley.

Desmond never went anywhere
without our Ghost Patrol business
cards. Even the beach!

That was when a flock of seagulls started circling our heads, squawking loudly and angrily. I groaned. At Dreary Beach, it's not the mersurfers you have to worry about . . . it's the seagulls!

Luckily, I was prepared. I took a deep breath and then emitted the highest-pitched screech I could make. **EEEEEEYYYYYAAAAA!**

My screech was so loud, both Desmond and Stanley had to cover their ears. The seagulls quickly scattered across the sky.

Stanley looked at me in amazement. "Whoa," he said. "How did you know that would work?"

"Seagulls are scared of hawks," I explained.

"Wow," Stanley said, looking from me to Desmond. "I've never met anyone cooler than you guys!"

CHAPTER THREE

THE SONG OF THE SUMMER

With the hot sun beating down on our heads, we decided it was time for a cold treat.

I guess everyone else at Dreary Beach had the same idea, because when the three of us got to the Snack Shack, the line was really long.

While we were waiting, we heard a loud humming noise over our heads. This time it wasn't the seagulls. A propeller plane was flying in the sky, pulling a long banner behind it. In big bold letters, the banner read: MINNIE & JIMMY ARE COMING TO KERSVILLE FOR THE CRAB POP!

I was confused. "Who are Minnie and Jimmy?" I asked. "And what's the Crab Pop?"

Stanley shrugged. "I have no idea."

A girl standing in front of us in line gasped. She turned around to look at us. "You don't know 'Crab Pop'? It's the number one hit song of the summer!"

Now it was my turn to shrug. I didn't listen to music all that much.

Just then a new song started playing through the Snack Shack's speakers. All the kids, including Desmond, seemed to know the lyrics.

"C'mon, everybody,
c'mon around!
C'mon, you know
this is gonna be a bop.
Put up your right claw,
put up your left one.
Now it's time to do the
Crab Pop!"

Desmond shuffled from side to side with the rest of the kids. They looked like dancing crabs.

Meanwhile, Stanley and I just stood there. Obviously, we were the only ones who didn't know "Crab Pop."

Once the song was over, we got to the front of the line and bought our shaved ices. Desmond and I walked back to our spot on the beach. Stanley tagged along with us too.

Mom pointed to the plane still flying overhead. "Would you boys like to see Minnie and Jimmy?" she asked us. "Our boss gave us free tickets to their concert."

My parents are scientists, and they work top secret jobs for the government. They get a lot of free stuff from their job. The stuff is usually really strange—one time, they brought home a box full of tiny snails! So, compared to that, free concert tickets were not so strange at all.

"No, thanks," Stanley and I both said. We'd never even heard of Minnie & Jimmy until a few minutes ago.

Mom turned to Desmond. "Maybe your parents can take you," she said.

"My parents are busy this week," Desmond said. He looked a little disappointed. But after a few more bites of shaved ice, he looked happy again.

When we finished eating, Stanley, Desmond, and I threw a beach ball around. Desmond dove face-first into the sand to catch the ball, and Stanley laughed until tears ran down his face.

My parents move around a lot for their jobs, so I knew what it felt like to be the new kid in town. The least I could do was make Stanley feel like he was welcome in Kersville.

CHAPTER FOUR

WILL YOU SIGN THIS?

The next day at school, Desmond and I were having a competition to see who could balance the longest on one foot. Seconds became minutes, and we were still balancing. My legs were shaking. Desmond's arms were flailing all over the place.

It finally ended when a hand tapped Desmond's shoulder, making him tip over.

"I win!" I shouted.

And then I saw who had tapped Desmond. It was Stanley! But there was something different about him.

He looked paler, his eyes looked wider, and . . . hmmm. There was something else different about him, but I couldn't quite figure it out.

"Hi, guys," Stanley said. "Guess what! We're playing Ghost Patrol!"

Stanley pointed across the play-ground, where a couple of other kids were running around.

One of them was wearing her jacket
hood. She was chasing the other kids
and moaning, **"Oooooooooh!"**

Desmond and I looked at each
other. Was the girl pretending to be
a ghost?

"Behold, my hawk screech!" Stanley
started chasing after the "ghost" and
screeching, **"EEEEEeeeeYYAAA!"**

Except he didn't sound anything like a hawk. Stanley sounded more like a baby goose!

Apparently it didn't matter what he sounded like. The girl gasped, "Oh no!" Then she covered her ears and fell to the ground dramatically.

Desmond shook his head. "Is that what they think the Ghost Patrol does?" he asked me.

"I hope not," I answered.

Stanley ran back over to us and held out the Ghost Patrol business card from yesterday. "Can I have your autographs?" he asked.

Desmond didn't hesitate. He pulled out a pen and signed the card, like it was something he did every day. Then he handed the card to me.

No one had ever asked me for my autograph before. I tried to sign my name as loopy as Desmond's, but I pressed the pen too hard, and I got a big ink blotch right in the middle of the card.

Ugh. How embarrassing!

Before we knew it, other kids from
the playground had gathered around
us. They all wanted autographed
business cards too.

There's something you should know about Desmond. He's always prepared for everything! So, of course, Desmond had a whole bunch of extra cards in his pockets.

Desmond and I signed cards for all the kids, and I didn't make any more ink blots! Everyone was so happy to get our autographs. You would have thought we were celebrities!

To be honest, it felt kind of fun to be famous on the playground.

Even if that feeling only lasted for a little while.

CHAPTER FIVE

THE SILENT TREATMENT

The next morning, Desmond was waiting for me outside his house. We always rode our bikes to school together.

But instead of hopping on his bike, Desmond motioned for me to follow him into his garage.

The Ghost Patrol headquarters is located in Desmond's garage, so I knew he had official business to discuss.

"What's going on?" I asked him. We usually didn't enter the headquarters until *after* school.

"Something weird is happening," Desmond said, pointing to the old-fashioned phone that used to belong to his grandmother. It was the Ghost Patrol hotline. Whenever there was a supernatural sighting, we received calls on it from kids all over Kersville.

"Weird like what?" I asked, staring at the phone. With Desmond, you weren't sure about what kind of weird he meant. Like, was the phone going to burst into flames or something?

The phone started ringing. That was what phones were supposed to do, so there wasn't anything weird about that.

Desmond picked it up and said, "Ghost Patrol. Desmond Cole speaking." Then he held out the phone so I could listen too.

No one responded. All we could hear was some static.

"This has been happening non-stop since yesterday," Desmond said. "There's never anyone on the other end."

Desmond hung up the phone. A few seconds later, it rang again. This time, I answered. "Hello, this is the Ghost Patrol," I said.

Again, there was nobody there. Just the same static. "Hello?" I repeated. "Hellllloooooooo?"

Nothing.

I hung up the phone, and it only took a couple of moments for it to start ringing. This time I had an idea.

"Hello," I said. "This is the . . . uh, the Pizza Store. If you tell us your name, we'll give you a free pizza!"

I was sure my trick would work, but nope. There was no response from the caller. Nothing but static.

Desmond was right. There was definitely something weird going on. I mean, who didn't want a free pizza?!

But we didn't have time to figure it out just yet. "C'mon," I said, hopping on my bike. "We're going to be late for school!"

Desmond unplugged the phone from the outlet so it would stop ringing. Then we started pedaling to school together.

"Do you think the kids from yesterday are prank calling us?" I asked Desmond as we zipped down the bike

lane. "We gave out all those Ghost Patrol business cards with our phone number on them."

"I don't think so," Desmond replied. "Would they really have the energy to stay up all night, just to call us for no reason?"

As we turned the corner to the school, I was convinced Desmond was right.

I ♥ GHOST PATROL

That was when we saw it, hanging right across the school building. It was the hugest banner I'd ever seen, and it read: I ♥ GHOST PATROL!

CHAPTER SIX

I Love the Ghost Patrol

Desmond and I braked our bikes and stood in front of the school, not sure what to do. Stanley was standing in front of the school doors. Maybe it was the light from the sun, but he looked even paler than he seemed yesterday.

Stanley practically squealed when he saw us. "Yay, you're here!" he said. He handed both of us pins from a huge box he was carrying.

I looked at the pin and gasped. It had a photo of Desmond and me, picking up the Ghost Patrol phone. The strange thing was . . . we were wearing the same clothes in the photo as we were wearing now!

I swallowed hard. "Um, Stanley," I began, "where did you get this photo?"

"Who's Stanley?" he answered. He put the box down, and that's when we could see that he was wearing a shirt that said GHOST PATROL FAN. "Call me Andmond!" he declared.

For a few seconds, Desmond looked as confused as I was, but then he snapped his fingers and said, "Oh, I get it. You combined 'And' from Andres and 'Mond' from Desmond, right?"

"Exactly!" Stanley said, beaming. "You're a genius!"

I stuffed the pin in my pocket. I couldn't tell if Stanley was being serious or if this was just some kind of joke.

Turns out, Stanley was dead serious! All day, he trailed us around the school.

During recess, he took out a ghost plushie from his backpack and used it like a puppet. "Desmond and Andres are my BEST friends!" the plushie said.

During lunch, he started taking photos with his camera. First it was a photo of the three of us. Then he started snapping photos of just Desmond and me.

Desmond was a natural in front of the camera. He didn't miss a beat, even when Stanley asked us to pose like werewolves and mummies.

Me? I was exhausted!

After lunch, I was relieved that Stanley was in a different class from us. Otherwise, I didn't think I would be able to pay attention.

But halfway through our math class, we realized it didn't matter. I glanced toward the classroom door and—**gulp!**—Stanley was spying on us through the window of the door!

I felt goose bumps on my arms. That boy was really creeping me out!

Our teacher, Dr. Ackula, opened the door and scolded Stanley for not

being in his own classroom. But all Stanley said was, "I only answer to the name Andmond."

At the end of the school day, I grabbed Desmond by the arm and we bolted out of the school—fast. The last thing we needed was Stanley, or Andmond, or *whatever* his name was, following us home!

CHAPTER SEVEN

LIVE FROM CHANNEL THIRTEEN

Desmond and I took the ziggiest, zaggiest route home. We passed Kersville Public Library, Kersville Museum, and even Kersville Stadium, which was crowded with a bunch of kids.

"Oh yeah!" Desmond said. "Today is the Minnie & Jimmy concert!"

A long line of kids was waiting to enter the stadium. Most of them were wearing matching T-shirts, and they were bouncing with excitement.

Suddenly there was a camera in front of my face. A big, fancy video camera.

"Hi, I'm Ivana Goodstory, reporting live from Channel Thirteen," a woman said, speaking toward the camera. "Today we're giving out free 'Crab Pop' goodies to lucky fans who can answer trivia questions about Minnie & Jimmy!"

Ivana Goodstory held out the microphone to me. "Are you ready for your question?"

"Oh, um," I began, feeling my heart beat superfast. "I'm not—"

Desmond nudged me in the ribs. The reporter was staring at me, impatiently tapping her foot. It seemed like the only way I could get out of this was to play along. "Okay," I said. "I'm ready."

"Great!" the reporter said, smiling widely for the camera. "Your first question is: How long have Minnie & Jimmy been performing music?"

Desmond started squirming. It was clear he knew the answer.

But I didn't!

"Um, two days?" I answered. I knew it was wrong, but *I* had only known about Minnie & Jimmy for two days. So that was my best guess.

"Sorry, kiddo!" the reporter replied. "That was a hard question, so let me give you another shot. Fill in the song lyrics: 'Put up your right claw, put up your left one. Now it's time to . . . ?'"

My mind went blank. How would I know those lyrics? I sighed and said the first thing that came to me. "'It's time to go home!'"

Desmond face-palmed next to me.
Even Ivana coughed, like she was
covering up a laugh. "Nice try!" she
said, but I knew she didn't mean it.
"The correct answer was 'do the
Crab Pop!'"

Oh. Of course! That was the song
playing at the Snack Shack the other
day.

Ivana cleared her throat.

"Okay, I'm going to give you one last chance," she said. "This should be a no-brainer." Then she started speaking slowly, as if that would help me answer. "How many people are in the group Minnie & Jimmy?"

The cameraperson zoomed in on my face, and I felt myself getting sweatier and sweatier. This was too much pressure! "I . . . uh . . . um . . ."

Finally, Desmond couldn't hold back anymore. "TWO!" he shouted. "Two people! MINNIE and JIMMY!"

"Correct!" Ivana exclaimed. "Well, your friend answered for you . . . but great job to your friend. And now for your prize!"

She reached into a large bag and gave me the floppiest straw hat I'd ever seen. Desmond got a bright red crab costume.

"Uh, thanks," I said, trying to sound excited.

As soon as the reporter left us to go interview someone else, I shoved the hat in my backpack. Then I told Desmond, "We'd better head home now." What if Stanley had been watching Channel Thirteen and saw us at the stadium?

That's when we heard someone call out, "Desmond! Andres!"

It was a voice we knew.

It was Stanley.

CHAPTER EIGHT

FLOATING ON AIR

There was only one thing we could do.

"RUN!" I yelled, dragging Desmond and our bikes as we weaved through the crowd.

We squeezed into a small space behind a ticket booth, hoping Stanley wouldn't see us.

"Wait!" I whispered. "I have an idea!" I unzipped my backpack and pulled out the floppy hat. I didn't think it would come in handy so soon.

Desmond whipped out his crab costume too—plus some sunglasses and a fake mustache. I had no idea why he would have those things, but it wasn't the time to ask!

So, now you know how Desmond and I ended up at Kersville Stadium wearing disguises, running away from the Ghost Patrol's number-one fan . . . who was taking things *way* too far!

It was hard to get through the crowd. Kids were everywhere, blocking every path we could take home. "Excuse me," we yelled, but nobody moved.

"Wait up!" We turned around and saw Stanley gaining on us! He saw right through our disguises. There was nowhere to go. There was no way to escape!

Stanley was getting closer and closer. Just before he was about to reach us, the crowd started shrieking with delight.

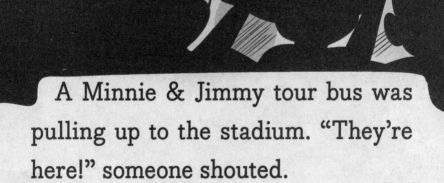

A Minnie & Jimmy tour bus was pulling up to the stadium. "They're here!" someone shouted.

Stanley froze in his tracks, turned toward the bus, and started cheering and waving frantically.

I looked at Desmond. "That's odd," I said. "I thought Stanley didn't know Minnie & Jimmy."

"If you think *that's* odd, look at what he's doing now!" Desmond pointed upward.

I looked up to see Stanley *floating* in the air! He hovered closer to the tinted windows of the bus. "Oh, now I can see them better!" Stanley exclaimed.

What was happening?!

Desmond and I watched Stanley as he floated to the ground with a dreamy look on his face. "I can't believe it," he said. "I got to see Minnie and Jimmy! We were so close. It was like we were breathing the same air! **WHEEEEEEE!**"

Stanley let out the longest and loudest squeal I'd ever heard. It was even longer and louder than the loudest hawk's screech.

Stanley's squeal was so long and so loud, all the lights went out.

Kersville Stadium was in a blackout!

CHAPTER NINE

SUPER PHANTOM

"Wow," Desmond whispered. He looked over at Stanley standing in the darkness. "That is one super phantom!"

"Phantom?" I whispered back. "You mean, Stanley is a ghost? Are you sure?"

I *did* just see him float into the air, and I was pretty sure he'd caused a blackout. But back at the beach, Stanley had seemed so confused about Kersville and the mersurfers. *That* didn't sound like a ghost to me.

"No, I don't think *Stanley* is a ghost," Desmond replied. "There's a *ghost* possessing Stanley's *body*!"

Whoa! I hadn't seen anything like that before!

Desmond approached Stanley and asked, "What's your name? Not Stanley, not Andmond, but your *real* name?"

When Stanley spoke, his voice sounded raspier. "You can call me Kipp," the ghost said.

He had possessed Stanley's body yesterday morning—which explained why Stanley had suddenly seemed so different. The boy we met at the beach didn't seem like someone who would hang up banners and sneak out of class to spy on us.

"Were you the one who called the hotline all night, too?" Desmond asked.

"Yeah," Kipp admitted. "But I get nervous talking on the phone." I could relate to that, even if I couldn't relate to calling someone *over* and *over*.

"I just needed to become best friends with you guys. By today!" Kipp said.

"Why?" Desmond asked.

"Well . . . ," Kipp said sheepishly. "I knew you had tickets for Minnie & Jimmy."

"Do you mean the free tickets my parents got from work?" I asked him.

"Yeah!" Kipp replied. "I heard you talking at the beach. Can you believe this guy turned those tickets down?" He pointed to Stanley's body. It was kind of confusing, because it looked like he was pointing to himself!

We had to do whatever it took to
get Stanley back. The *real* Stanley!

"If we let you see the concert, will
you promise to unpossess Stanley?"
I asked Kipp.

Kipp nodded. "I promise to leave Stanley's body as soon as we are finished doing the Crab Pop."

So we parked our bikes and walked to the ticket booth. Luckily, there were three tickets reserved for Miedoso.

Desmond looked over at the stadium entrance, which was still pitch-black. "Kipp, you have to turn the power back on. Otherwise there won't be a concert."

Kipp's shoulders slumped. "But I don't know how to turn the lights back on," he said.

"What are we going to do?" I asked Desmond. "If we don't get the lights back on, they're probably going to cancel the whole concert. And if we can't do the Crab Pop, then we can't get Stanley back!"

Desmond took the tickets from my hand and looked at them. That was when I saw a smile on his face. "Hey, Kipp. Did you know these are *front-row* tickets?"

Kipp's eyes flew open larger than dinner plates. He was so excited, we had to grab on to his arms to keep him from floating off into outer space. "Did you just say . . . FRONT ROW TICKETS?????" he screeched.

BZZZZZZZZ.

Suddenly the lights popped back on! Everybody cheered as they made their way into the stadium. Desmond and I breathed a sigh of relief. That wasn't so hard after all.

With any luck, it was going to be
just as easy to get Stanley back too!

CHAPTER TEN

DO THE CRAB POP

Once we were inside, we took our seats in the front row.

There was a paper fan on every seat, and kids were already waving them around excitedly. So was Kipp! Desmond looked happy to be at the concert too.

To be honest, I still didn't care about seeing the concert. But I didn't want to bum anyone out. Especially if that anyone was a phantom.

After a while, the lights dimmed. The audience started cheering. Over the loudspeakers, a voice boomed, "ARE! YOU! READY?!"

"YEESSSS!" the crowd screamed.

Minnie & Jimmy appeared onstage and, man, did the crowd go wild— especially Kipp.

I never knew phantoms could be such big fans!

As the music filled the stadium, I sat there, waiting for them to sing "Crab Pop" so Kipp could unpossess Stanley and we could go home.

But then, believe it or not, with every song Minnie & Jimmy sang, I got into their music a little more. They had so much talent and so much energy! It was all really contagious.

"MINNIE & JIMMY *ARE* KIND OF AWESOME!" I said to Desmond, screaming over the music.

"I knew you'd get it eventually!" he screamed back.

Soon, Minnie & Jimmy were singing the last song of the night. And of course, they saved the best for last. It was finally time to do the Crab Pop!

Desmond, Kipp, and I waved our peace signs and sang along. The words repeated a lot, so they weren't all that difficult to learn!

Kipp turned to us with happy tears in his eyes. "That was amazing! It was everything I wanted!"

Desmond and I watched as the phantom exited Stanley's body.

Nobody else seemed to notice though. They were too busy watching Minnie & Jimmy throw kisses at the crowd.

Kipp was still hovering over the audience when Stanley blinked a few times.

"What? Where am I?" Stanley asked, looking around at all the cheering kids. When he looked up and saw Kipp, he gasped.

Kipp waved shyly. "Sorry . . . and thank you," he said before floating off into the sky.

"Whoa! Was that a phantom? Did it just apologize to me?" Stanley asked. He shook his head. "This town is so WEIRD!"

The real Stanley was back!

"It *is* weird," I said, putting a hand on his shoulder. "But don't worry. You'll get used to it."

Stanley nodded. "And if anything happens, I have this." He pulled out the Ghost Patrol business card from his pocket, the one with Desmond's signature and my ink blotch!

"The Ghost Patrol is always here to help," I said.

Desmond added, "Just don't call the hotline ALL NIGHT LONG!"

Stanley looked puzzled. "Why would I do that?" he asked.

"It's a looong story," Desmond said. Right now, we had something more important to do—sing along to the encore of "Crab Pop"!

To
Luke,
Merry Christmas!
Love,

Grandma Cathy - 2021

'Twas the night before Christmas,
when all through the house,
Not a creature was stirring,
not even a mouse;
Luke's stocking was hung
by the chimney with care,
In hope that St. Nicholas
soon would be there.

Luke was nestled all snug in his bed,
While visions of candy canes danced in his head.
And Mom in her kerchief, and Dad in his cap,
Had just settled down for a long winter's nap.

When out on the street
there arose such a clatter,
Luke sprang from his bed
to see what was the matter.
Away to the window
Luke flew like a flash,
Tore open the curtains,
threw open the latch.

The moon on the blanket
of new-fallen snow,
Shone bright as midday
on the objects below—

When, what to Luke's
wondering eyes should appear,
But a miniature sleigh
and eight tiny reindeer.

With a little old driver,
so lively and quick,
Luke knew in a moment
it must be St. Nick.
More rapid than eagles
his reindeer they came,
And he whistled, and shouted,
and called them by name:

To
Luke

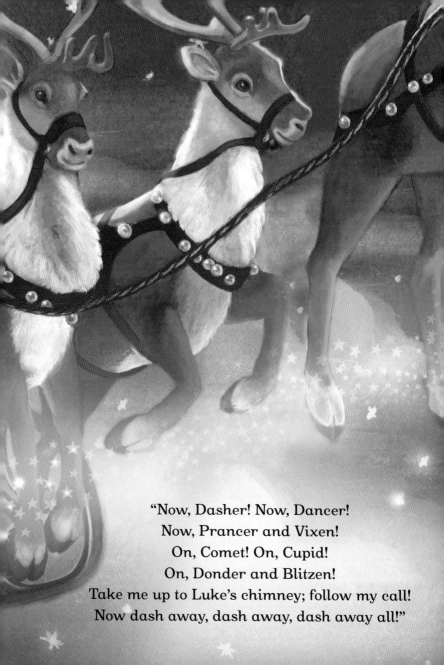

"Now, Dasher! Now, Dancer!
Now, Prancer and Vixen!
On, Comet! On, Cupid!
On, Donder and Blitzen!
Take me up to Luke's chimney; follow my call!
Now dash away, dash away, dash away all!"

And then, in a twinkling,
Luke heard on the roof
The prancing and pawing
of each little hoof.

As Luke pulled in his head
and was turning around,
Down the chimney
St. Nicholas came with a bound.

He was dressed all in fur,
from his head to his foot,
And his clothes were all tarnished
with ashes and soot.
A bundle of toys he had
flung on his back,
And he looked like a peddler
holding his pack.

To
Luke

His eyes—how they twinkled!
His dimples—how merry!
His cheeks were like roses,
his nose like a cherry.
His droll little mouth
was drawn up like a bow,
And the beard on his chin was
as white as the snow.

Dear Santa,
I hope you enjoy the sweet treats.
Love,
Luke
P.S. The carrots are for your furry friends.

A big sack of toys
he held tight in his fist,
And he glanced to see Luke
at the top of his list.
He had a broad face
and a little round belly
That shook when he laughed,
like a bowl full of jelly.

NICE LIST

Luke

Steven

Glenn

Marcus

Lorenzo

Luke

He was chubby and plump,
a right jolly old elf,
And Luke laughed when he saw him,
in spite of himself.

St. Nick winked an eye
and tilted his head
Letting Luke know
he had nothing to dread.

He spoke not a word,
but went straight to his work,
And filled up Luke's stocking,
then turned with a jerk.

And tapping his finger at the side of his nose,
And giving a nod, up the chimney he rose.

He sprang to his sleigh, to his team gave a whistle,
And away they all flew like the down of a thistle.
But St. Nicholas exclaimed, as he drove out of sight—

Luke, draw all your favorite
Christmas presents from Santa.

Adapted from the poem by Clement C. Moore
Illustrated by Lisa Alderson
Designed by Jane Gollner

Copyright © Bidu Bidu Books Ltd 2021

Published by Put Me In The Story,
a publication of Sourcebooks, Inc.
P.O. Box 4410, Naperville, Illinois 60567-4410
(630) 536-1104
www.putmeinthestory.com

Date of Production: June 2021
Run Number: 5022128
Printed and bound in Italy (LG)
10 9 8 7 6 5 4 3

FSC
www.fsc.org

MIX
Paper from
responsible sources
FSC® C023419

put me in the story

Bestselling books starring your child!
www.putmeinthestory.com